TO ME WAY-AY-AY-YAH!

We'll all throw dirt at the cook!

from the short-drag chantey "Paddy Doyle"

from the fo'c'sle ballad "The Boston Come-All-Ye"

Come, all ye young sailormen, listen to me,

I'll sing you a song of the fish of the sea.

Then blow ye winds westerly, westerly blow,

WE'RE BOUND TO THE SOUTH-.'ARD,

SO STEADY SHE GOES!

LOUD EMILY

ALEXIS O'NEILL

PICTURES BY

NANCY CARPENTER

ALADDIN PAPERBACKS

NEW YORK   LONDON   TORONTO   SYDNEY   SINGAPORE

For David, my WZRDJG, with all my love
(and with thanks to all the Emilys)

—A.O.

In honor of all the unknown artists of the nineteenth century,
and for Gia, certain to be a well-known artist
of the next century

—N.C.

First Aladdin Paperbacks edition December 2001
Text copyright © 1998 by Alexis O'Neill
Illustrations copyright © 1998 by Nancy Carpenter

ALADDIN PAPERBACKS
An imprint of Simon & Schuster Children's Publishing Division
1230 Avenue of the Americas, New York, NY 10020

Also available in a SIMON & SCHUSTER BOOKS FOR YOUNG READERS hardcover edition.
Designed by Heather Wood. The text of this book was set in Cheltenham.
The illustrations were rendered in oil paint.
Printed in Hong Kong
2 4 6 8 10 9 7 5 3 1

The Library of Congress has cataloged the hardcover edition as follows:
O'Neill, Alexis, 1949-
Loud Emily / written by Alexis O'Neill ; illustrated by Nancy Carpenter.
p.   cm.
Summary : A little girl with a big voice who lives in a nineteenth-century whaling town
finds a way to be useful and happy aboard a sailing ship.
ISBN 0-689-81078-4 (hc.)
[1. Voice—Fiction. 2. Sea stories.] I. Carpenter, Nancy, ill. II. Title
PZ7.O5523Lo   1998   [E]—dc21   97-18217
ISBN 0-689-84669-X (Aladdin pbk.)

The songs on the endpapers and others like them can be found in *Songs of the American Sailormen* by Joanna C. Colcord
(W.W. Norton & Co., Inc., 1938) and *The Music of the Waters* by Laura Alexandrine Smith (Kegan Paul, Trench & Co., 1888).

SAILORS' TERMS AND PHRASES

Ahoy!
Attention!

All hands on deck!
Everyone must come up to the top platform of the ship!

Avast!
Stop what you're doing!

Aye, aye!
Yes!

bosun (boatswain)
whistle-carrying officer in charge of deck crew

bowsprit
pole extending forward from the ship

cooper
person who makes wooden barrels

chantey
song sung by sailors to the rhythm of their movements while working
Different kinds of chanteys—short-drag, capstan, and halyard—
were sung for different kinds of work.

fo'c'sle (forecastle)
section of the upper deck located at the front of the ship
A fo'c'sle ballad is a story sung when the crew was off-duty.

Furl the main and stop it down!
Roll up the main sail and tie it down with short lines of rope!

halyard
rope for hoisting or lowering a sail or a flag
"Blow the Man Down" is a famous halyard chantey.

Luff her up before we're stove!
Steer our ship into the wind so the sails flap, or else we'll crash!

mizzenmast
third mast back on a sailing ship

quarter-deck
back part of a sailing ship, usually reserved for officers

rigger
person who fits a system of ropes, chains, and tackles used
to support masts, sails, and yards of a sailing vessel

smithy
person who works in a blacksmith shop, making items
out of iron with an anvil and a hammer

swabbing
mopping

tiller
lever used to turn a rudder and steer a ship

From the moment of birth Emily's voice boomed.

"GOO GOO BA BA!" Emily sang in her Emily voice.

It startled the midwife. It astonished the neighbors. It frightened the birds that were nesting in trees.

Emily's parents loved her truly, but oh, dear! Her voice could be heard 'round that seaside town!

"Perhaps she'll grow out of it," said her father as he closed all the windows and fastened the doors.

"We can only hope," said her mother as she covered her ears with embroidered pillows.

But as Emily grew, so did her voice. It rattled the brasses. It shimmied the crystals. It shattered the plates as they crashed to the floor.

"GOOD MORNING!" Emily said in her Emily voice.

"Please be soft," said Father.

"GOOD AFTERNOON!" Emily said in her Emily voice.

"Please do whisper," said Mother.

"I'M READY FOR LESSONS!" Emily said in her Emily voice.

"You *must* be *quiet*," snapped the tutor, who threatened to quit.

When Emily turned seven, she heard Father fretting, "How will she find her way in the world?"

Mother sighed, "How will she find friends?"

The tutor hissed, "How can I teach such a boisterous child?"

"I'LL TRY HARDER," Emily vowed in her Emily voice. Emily slipped back into the hallway. Her lonely footsteps echoed on the polished floor. She wandered past the grand staircase and tiptoed down by the in-and-out door. Emily tweaked it open a crack. Oh! She heard pots and pans banging, cupboard doors slamming, errand boys yelling, "Deliveries ho!"

Emily stepped inside and tugged at the skirts of the kitchen's round cook.

"MAY I HELP YOU?" Emily asked in her Emily voice.

"How grand! A lass who speaks up!" said the cook above the happy din. "Call the servants for tea, please."

"TEA TIME!" Emily called up the dumbwaiter. The inside servants came running. "CRUMPETS AND SCONES FOR EVERYONE!" she called out the garden door.

The cook beamed. "What a fine help you are, little Emily." So Emily helped in the kitchen every morning.

Upstairs, her parents still worried.

"What about a boarding school?" her father wondered.

"A boarding school?" her mother asked.

"Yes, she must go to a boarding school," crowed the tutor, "far across the sea! And may I suggest Miss Meekmeister's School for Soft-Spoken Girls?"

Emily tried to be happy. But a misty greyness crept inside her and would not go away.

On the day before Emily was to set sail, the cook took her hand. "Come, little Emily. Before you go, come with me to Front Street and help me buy some nice fresh fish."

Emily heard Front Street before she saw it. Oh! What a lovely place it was, there among the tall ships. The salty air rang with the sounds of riggers and smithies and coopers at work. Sailors trundled cargo along wooden wharves. Carriages thundered up cobblestone streets. Crowds burst from taverns with songs on their lips.

"I LOVE IT HERE!" Emily said in her Emily voice. As Emily skipped along the wharf, she saw a small notice tacked to a large ship.

LOUD HELP NEEDED.
NOW.
CASTING OFF TODAY.
Captain Baroo

"Ahoy there," called the first mate to Emily. "Are you loud?"

"I AM!" answered Emily.

"Come aboard, then," he said.

And Emily did.

She walked up the rickety plank and right into Captain Baroo.

"MY NAME IS EMILY," Emily said in her Emily voice.
"HOW CAN I HELP?"

"Can you call an order from the fo'c'sle to quarter-deck above a gale force wind?" peeped Captain Baroo.

"AYE AYE, CAPTAIN!" she said.

Before the captain could say "Mizzenmast," Emily called, "ALL HANDS ON DECK!" and every ship's crew came running.

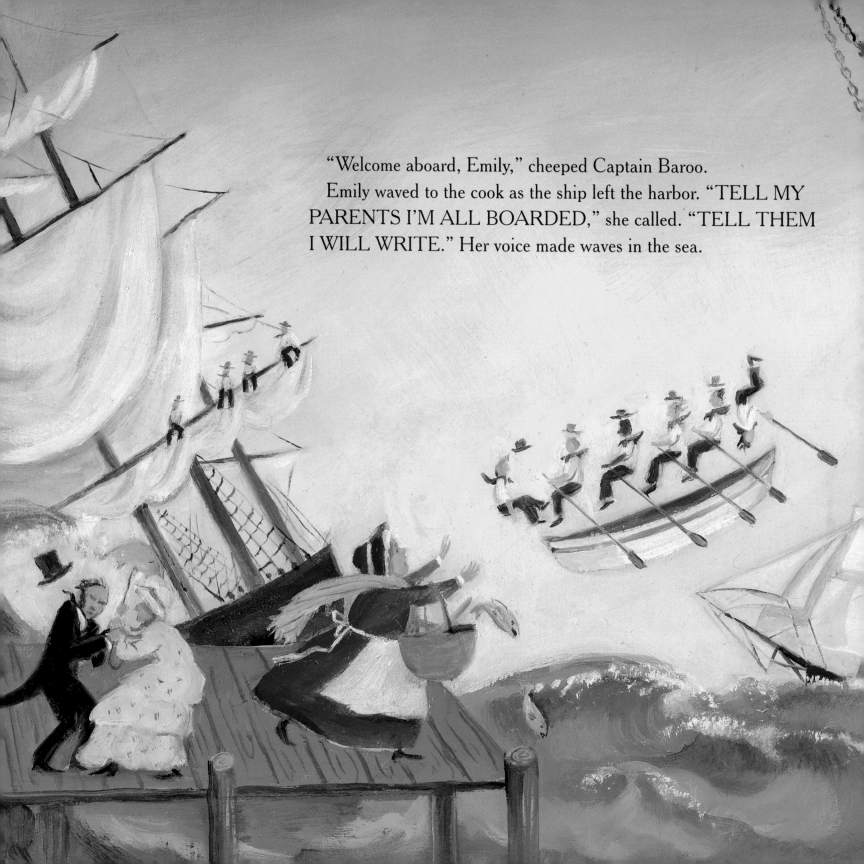

"Welcome aboard, Emily," cheeped Captain Baroo.

Emily waved to the cook as the ship left the harbor. "TELL MY PARENTS I'M ALL BOARDED," she called. "TELL THEM I WILL WRITE." Her voice made waves in the sea.

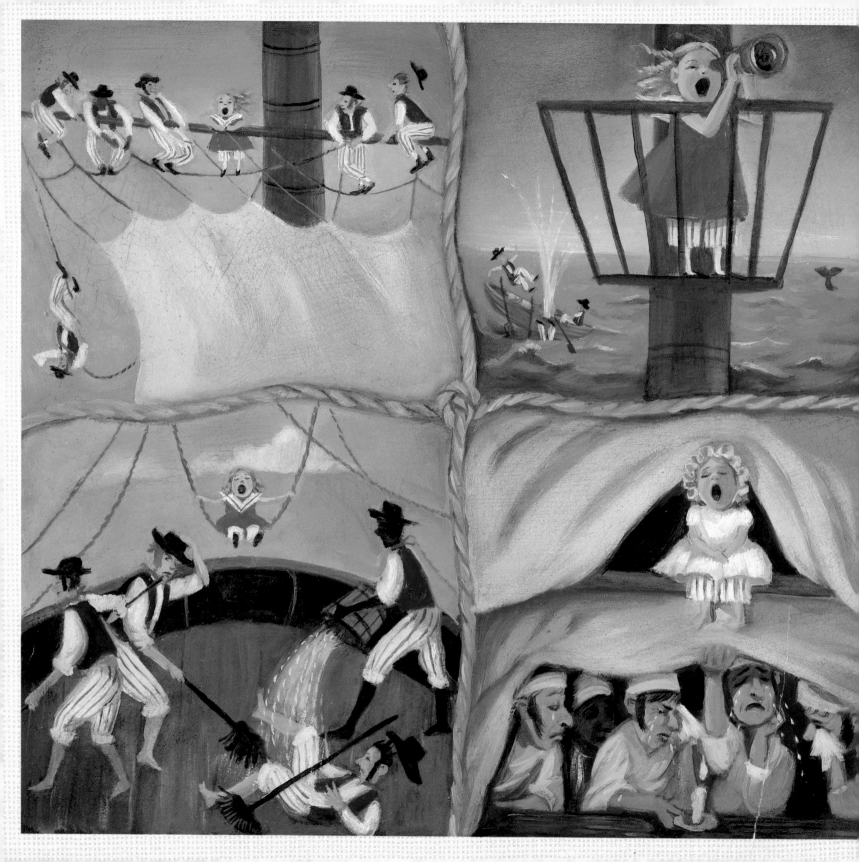

Captain Baroo's crew was kind and luckless. But how they loved Emily's voice! She sang halyard chanteys while hoisting the sails. She called bosun's commands while standing the watch. She told stories to the crew while swabbing the deck. From her tidy bunk at night she crooned fo'c'sle ballads that made the men cry.

And deep out in the ocean the whales listened, too. They danced to her wild tunes. They sang with her free songs. They spouted and blew their delight in the air.

One day, a storm lifted waves into walls of water and shivered the timbers of the very old ship. Captain Baroo whispered commands into Emily's ear.

Emily shouted, "AVAST! LUFF HER UP BEFORE WE'RE STOVE!"

The men scrambled into the riggings as the ship pitched and plunged and dove into the raging sea.

She cried, "FURL THE MAIN AND STOP IT DOWN!"

The wind screamed its fury as Captain Baroo and his raggedy crew rolled up the sails. All day and all night they fought the wild and thundering waves. They kept the ship safe until the storm finally moved on. "At last." The captain sighed.

But when morning came, fog rolled in like a blanket of blubber.
"Can't see a thing!" complained Captain Baroo.
"Neither can we!" moaned his poor tired crew, and they fell fast
asleep on the deck.
Emily peered over the railing.

Rocks! The ship was racing fast toward a rough, jagged shore.
Where was the lighthouse? Had the fierce storm destroyed it?

"AHOY!" Emily called in her Emily voice. "AHOY! AHOY!"
But nothing could wake the snoring crew. She pulled at the tiller but
the ship wouldn't turn. What could she do?

And then she remembered the whales.

Emily rushed to the bowsprit and shimmied along. Into the waves
she cast her voice until a ribbon of bubbles carried her words into the
briny deep: "DANGER! PLEASE HELP! DANGER! PLEASE
HELP!" She sang in song for the whales. And as Emily sang, the
whales gathered 'round. They hastened from Baja, they raced down
from Iceland, they speeded their way from the tip of Cape Horn. Then,
as if the ship were one of their own, they nuzzled her and cradled her
and eased her away from the treacherous coast.

Emily sighed. Safe! But the other ships from the seaside town . . .
they faced danger, too. So she called once again to her friends of the
sea. Between rolling waves and hazardous rocks the whales formed
a long bridge, the whales formed a wide bridge, and Emily ran from
her ship to the shore. Up the winding lighthouse stairs she scrambled
and took her deepest, deepest breath.

"DaaaaaaaanGER! ROCKS heeeeeere!" she called.

"Rocks HEEEEEEEERE! DAAAAANger!"

Over and over she sang her two-note warning:

"DaaaaaaaanGER! ROCKS heeeeeere!"

"Rocks HEEEEEEEERE! DAAAAANger!"

Emily's voice rang out loud and true. Her call pierced the thick fog, her voice tamed the fierce waves, and the captains and crews turned their ships back to sea.

Soon the sun shone in the wide sky. On the horizon were ships and ships and ships, far from the threatening rocks. Along the shore stood all the folks of the city shouting HURRAH! for the little girl with the very big voice. The happiest shouts of all came from her own proud parents.